Eustace
& Clyde

Marina Aizen
Dallas Public Library

Sky Pony Press
New York

This is Clyde.

This is Eustace.

Clyde is no ordinary koala.
He doesn't like leaves.
He has no time for lazing on branches.
And he never sleeps during the day.

Eustace is no ordinary koala either.
Sometimes he eats too many leaves.
Sometimes he loves lazing on branches.
And sometimes he sleeps all day.

Clyde and Eustace share a home.

They care about each other very much.

Although sharing can be
a bit tricky sometimes.

Hyde and Eustace longed for a place of their own.
It wasn't that they disliked company.
But sometimes, it was better to be just two.

"A home that is just ours," said Clyde.
"That's what we need."

So Clyde and Eustace set out in search of
the perfect place for a koala pair.

"This place is excellent!" said Clyde.

"Um, Clyde—I think it might be taken," replied Eustace.

"This is so much fun!" said Eustace.

"Oh! I think it is too dangerous!" said Clyde.

"Look, Eustace! This place is HUGE!"

"Clyde, the breeze is so lovely!"
"But Eustace, it's too hot!"

"Eustace, we can make snowmen!"
"But Clyde, it's too cold!"

"Eustace, we have plenty of space!"
"Yes Clyde, but it's so far away..."

"Clyde! What a wonderful view!"
"Eustace! It's far too close to the city..."

"Do you think we might have made a mistake?" said Clyde.

"Maybe there is nowhere we can be just two?" said Eustace.

CHIRP

SQUAWK

SQUEAK

"Although maybe there is one place
we could take another look at?"

"And maybe it is closer than we think!"

It might be crowded and a bit noisy sometimes...
But wherever they have each other is the perfect place for a koala pair!

For Toto, Joaco, Dad and Mark, four very
special gentlemen in my life and heart.
And to all my readers, I hope you enjoy
walking with these two little friends.

– Marina Aizen

First Sky Pony Press edition, 2017

Sky Pony Press books may be purchased in bulk at special discounts for sales promotion, corporate gifts, fund-raising, or educational purposes. Special editions can also be created to specifications. For details, contact the Special Sales Department, Sky Pony Press, 307 West 36th Street, 11th Floor, New York, NY 10018 or info@skyhorsepublishing.com.

Sky Pony® is a registered trademark of Skyhorse Publishing, Inc.®, a Delaware corporation.
Visit our website at www.skyponypress.com.

10 9 8 7 6 5 4 3 2 1

Manufactured in China, January 2017
This product conforms to CPSIA 2008

Library of Congress Cataloging-in-Publication Data is available on file.

Cover illustration credit Marina Aizen

Print ISBN: 978-1-5107-1502-8
Ebook ISBN: 978-1-5107-1503-5